# What Will You Be For Halloween?

**GLORIA GARDNER**

Illustrations by Robyn Hodgdon

LUMINARE PRESS

WWW.LUMINAREPRESS.COM

Printed in the United States of America

Illustrations by Robyn Hodgdon
Cover and Interior Design by Melissa K. Thomas

Luminare Press
442 Charnelton St.
Eugene, OR 97401
www.luminarepress.com

LCCN: 2020914315
ISBN: 978-1-64388-431-8

*This book is dedicated to everyone who loves Halloween,*
*both the young and old, alike. Halloween fills us with unforgettable,*
*fun memories of surprises, mysteries and trick or treating adventures.*
*Especially remembered are the costume choices that we made for Halloween.*
*With so many possible choices, did we choose to look silly or scary or beautiful?*
*And because of our excitement about Halloween, we often ask each other,*
*"What will you be for Halloween?"*

What will you be for Halloween?

A football player who tackles and throws?

Or a crab with pincers that open and close?

Or a ballerina dancing girl,

Who can leap and stretch and twist and twirl?

Or a baker with cookies and sweet things to eat?

Or a knight on the lookout for dragons to meet?

Which costume will you choose?

Or does it just confuse?

Will you be a pumpkin, big and orange and round?

Or a witch on a broom taking off from the ground?

Or a playful black cat?

Or a wizard with a tall, pointy hat?

How about that?

4

Will you be a robot with a jerky walk,

And a deep, deep voice that makes strange talk?

Or an astronaut who can zoom through space?

Or a runner who's ready to enter a race?

Or a happy clown with a painted face?

Sometimes it's hard to make up your mind,

And choose the costume you want to find.

Do you want to be a vampire with fangs that can bite?

Or a ghost that says "boo" and floats in the night?

Or a pirate who's holding a treasure chest?

Or a cowgirl riding her horse out West?

Which one of these would you like best?

How about a fairy who makes wishes come true?

Or an alien with a laser gun shooting glue?

Or a spooky goblin who can fool and trick?

Or a soccer ball player who can run and kick?

Which one will you pick?

Will you choose to be a spider, all fuzzy and black

With eight wiggly legs that crawl forward and back?

Or a martial arts master who breaks wood with a whack?

Or a princess dressed in a fancy, pink gown,

Happily wearing a sparkly, jeweled crown?

Or how about T-Rex, who's both mighty and brave?

Or a furry brown bear just out of his cave?

It's not easy to pick which one.

But don't you agree, it's really fun?

You might be a mermaid who swims in the sea,

Or maybe dress up like a bumblebee.

You might be a lion, very proud of your mane,

Or a conductor who helps travelers get onto the train.

Can you pick your favorite one?

Are you still thinking? Or are you done?

Won't it be fun to surprise us all,

Whether you fly or walk or crawl,

Whether you hoot or howl or chase,

Whether you wear a scary mask or a funny, clown face,

Whether you dance or bake or sing,

Whether you're a robot or a king,

Whether you're a pirate with a patch upon your eye,

Whether you're silly or brave or cute as pie,

It will be fun! You can count on that!

By now, I hope you know what you'll be.

I'm ready for a surprise! And I can't wait to see!

TRICK OR TREAT

# SILLY FUN!

**What's scarier than seeing T-Rex?**
Being chased by T-Rex

**If a witch invites you to ride with her on her broom,**
**what could you say?**
"I'll be right back. Let me go ask my mom, first."

**What does a ghost say?**
"Boo"

**What does a ghost say when he's hurting?**
"Boo-hoo"

**If you dress up as "he-man", and your sister wants to**
**be one, too, then what would she be called?**
"She-man"?

**Are bumblebees pretty?**
Yes, they're pretty busy, they're pretty buzzy, and they're pretty ouchy.

**If you're an astronaut, and you're traveling to the moon on Halloween,**
**what should you remember to take with you?**
Your trick-or-treat bag

**What kind of cat doesn't want to go riding**
**on a broom stick with a witch?**
A Scaredy Cat

# DO YOU KNOW?

Which small Halloween character can scare you when
its eight fuzzy legs start to crawl on you?
A Spider

Which Halloween character lives in the ocean and swishes her long,
beautiful fish tail when she swims?
A Mermaid

Which Halloween character plays on a team and can kick
the ball down the field to score a goal?
A Soccer Player

Which Halloween character is soft and black and furry and
rides with the witch on a broom stick?
A Black Cat

Which Halloween character lives in a castle and wears a fancy,
pink gown and a sparkly, jeweled crown?
A Princess

Which Halloween character wears a loose, white sheet
and looks at you through its two, big eyes?
A Ghost

Which Halloween character lives in the ocean and has a
hard shell, eight legs, and two pincers?
A Crab

# WHAT DO YOU THINK?

Is there a Halloween costume that you think looks really scary?

If a fairy could make a wish come true for you,
what would you want it to be?

If you were a pirate, can you think of a good
hiding place for your treasure?

Can you think of something you could do to make a clown laugh?

Wizards know lots of things, but what is something
that a wizard doesn't know about you?

What kind of a sweet treat would you love for a baker to make for you?

Can you think of some magic words that a witch might say when
she wants her broom to start flying her up into the air?

Made in the USA
Monee, IL
21 October 2020